Stranded on Love's Highway

Kefentse Booth

Printed in the United States of America

ISBN 978-0-9977409-2-9

eBook ISBN 978-0-9977409-3-6

Published by Street Light Dreams, LLC, Detroit, MI
www.StreetLightDreams.com

This book is dedicated to my Glover, Boykins, and
Booth family

Table of Contents

Preface

She's gone! I get that, but the days seem long and the nights whisper seductive nothings into my lonely bedroom. I stare out my bedroom windows, trying to find images of hope. I leave my sanity in the vision of my eyesight instead of in my mind and heart. I am treading on thin ice. I am starting to understand the world without me.

Sure, I see my value; but the mirror is reflecting someone I've never seen before. Love hurts, but time isn't curing this hole in my chest. I wonder about her, only at moments when my life replays memories of time spent. The radio can go to hell in a handbasket. The TV is programmed to that channel and shows that connected our personalities. The winds tantalize me with a scent that hints her aura.

Am I chasing reality or falling into depression? Am I better alone or without breath? I wondered how love could allow someone to take their life because *love* didn't love back in the same manner they loved the other. Well today, I understand. I understand the feeling of wanting them to call when you know they've erased your number. The search for a touch that doesn't extend their reach to help pick you up in this time of need.

I thought we were best friends. Damn near till death do us part. The lies that were told--and all for what? To have a deeper connection in a soul that wouldn't attach forever. To make believe that the "I love you" meant something as I deepened my boat anchor into her abyss. The way we stared into each other's eyes with admiration, only to find a wick smoking with no flame.

That's it! We were the fire the bystanders needed to see to believe in love—only to show them that love, true love, doesn't exist in the world we created. Was the wool pulled over my eyes? Did you love me like you claimed? Hell, now I'm questioning if I loved *you* as deep as my mouth uttered. Wounds hurt, and no bullet or knife feels like this piercing desire.

I gave you the world that I was able to provide. I gave you my all, in the midst of not knowing I had more. I saw more for us, yet time saw the end, I guess. Sure, my life was nestled in compartments that needed action individually. I was getting around to opening those corridors to my soul. Standoffish and introverted, I think it is called, but nevertheless, I feel misunderstood in this world. It was easy to give to you because it was easy to understand you. I guess I was a walking labyrinth, an oil-painted enigma with water damage—or simply the key that didn't fit your lock to forever.

Maybe I'll drink my pain away. Find a nice bottle of something and backstroke in our memories, until I crash on some deserted island. That should ease the burden. Drown my liver until the poison subdues my mobility, and then play in traffic like a squirrel trying to cross a busy interstate. Maybe I should smoke until my lungs are clouded with the gray skies of my existence. I should smoke until the hallucinogen attacks my mental.

Still, I know I am better than this. I have to focus on tomorrow because right now is killing me softly. If only there was a way to stand upright and get out this bed. I need to find a way to stare in the mirror of life and command greatness. If I found love once, surely I can find love again. But wait, maybe that was it. Maybe I gave my all to someone that didn't love the *love* I seek. Maybe I'm trying to control a love that is greater than any I've ever experienced. Maybe my great lies in the understanding that help is needed.

Where did my faith go in this process? Ask and it shall be given, correct? Well, I want out of this purgatory in which I reside in. I want to be led to love instead of finding and molding it. Give me someone I can grow with. I need someone that can see through my eyes and see my soul, someone who can truly understand the heavens from which I have come from.

Give me a love that I will live for and die for because the breath they hold is the breath that inhabits my lungs. Sew my wound up and complete me again. Strengthen me so she sees a strong man who's nothing like the boys that run behind her. I am ready for what's next. I just have to purge the old out of my life for good. Time to look past the clouds and through them for the sunshine I know is on the other side someday.

Stranded

The world is revolving. Day into night, night into day. I lounged in my soul while my shell rested in the world. I nestled my faith in a cold room with blanketed, "Goodnights!" My soul longed for nothing because my soul was lost in an unwanted crevice.

I was damaged. Involved in an accident that shredded me. Where was love? Where did it go? With tears in my eyes, I'm flying down the interstate, searching for it. Yet, my car isn't fast enough. I was outrun and left without navigation. I understood now. Love was gone!

Staring out my rearview, at the memories that seemed larger than my windshield, the city lights faded in the distance as I drove to God only knows where. I'm definitely unfocused. I count the lines in the road as I begin to veer into the opposite lane. The honking from semi-trucks gets my attention right before death gets my soul. This monotony has me asking 'what if' scenarios that won't help bring you back.

I think I'm lost. Alone in a world that I once traveled with happiness. Yet, confused at my surroundings; nothing looks familiar. Where am I? Both physically and mentally, I seek direction. The horizon is setting and my world is drawing to a close. Another night is upon me and I have no one to say, "Good night!" to. No one to hold and protect as our dreams play out past the midnight hour. The stars peek into the dark night, twinkling and awaiting vessels to make wishes in the air of the night.

My headlights are on and my mind is in a seductive trance. I powered off the radio. One more love song, and I was bound to release tears. Hours passed and I aimlessly cruised. It's been days and yet, I aimlessly continue to look for you. But have you looked for me like I hunt for you? Do you question my wellbeing like I've concerned myself with yours?

This sorrow is too much! I should give up and head back home. Back to that place of familiarity and recognizable nothingness. Maybe I'll jimmy the lock on my corridor doors. It must be someone I trust to help me. Or maybe I'll self-diagnose and counsel myself. How hard could it be? I just need to love all of myself first, then explore for love, like a search party rescue mission.

I need to pull over. These thoughts are too heavy on my mind. On the side of a interstate, I sit, clinching a gift you once gave me. I am completely done! I rest our memories on the side of Mile Marker 143. Maybe your next love will find the piece of your heart I once held. Surely, you needed someone to love you deeper than the depth I had to give.

It's serene tonight, with a calm air. I look toward home in the distance. I think I'll walk. Plus, this vessel has run out of gas. In the backdrop, I hear buzzards squawk. They anticipate my last breath. I'm stranded on love's highway. Alone on this path, trying to find myself. After several miles, the sun speaks to me. It's a new day. It's a new life.

I'll look for love again sooner or later as I finally walk away from my past.

The Farmer and the Fruit

The grounds are fertile, seeded lands with enrichment to strengthen roots that grow. Feeble structures of plants round their core out and grow lines to show age within the trunk of groomed trees. Seasonal alterations over the years have allowed the bark to harden and protect the molecules that helped bear fruit of sensual taste. The piercing of teeth into the skin of this fruit secretes the warmest of nectars; the welcoming aura of delight, joy held in the hands of the holder.

Amazing in form, the recipient analyzes the tree, hoping this offspring can reproduce the love they just found through the planting of the seeds, which are still attached to the core. Planting, he does; so he labors to dig the trench that will house the plant which grows into the tree that will spawn the fruit for him to eat. Anticipating the arrival of the harvest, he stares out the window in his home as the spring season brings buds to the branches. Leaves now expand and fold out with fuzzy buds that house the zygotes of the soon-to-be nourishment.

The day has come. The makeshift farmer understands that in the harvest, there is only one fruit that can be reproduced and all elements have to be right for the evolution to be supreme. He grants his watering mouth another day to let it hang on the branch for extra ripeness. The farmer approaches his prized possession, anticipating the connection of the lips to the skin, the slow penetration of teeth to insides, the slow swallow of juices as the seepage trickles down his esophagus. He stands before his tree, yet sees no fruit. Like a thief in the night, someone has stolen his joy.

Hysterical in movement, he ponders the happening. With no conclusion that can be met, he wanders the countryside. To his avail, he finds the fruit half the distance away from the tree, which he once picked. He leans over and picks it up. Thinking the breeze during the night must have blown it away, he closes his eyes and opens his mouth for their passionate kiss. Teeth sinking in, his lips feel rough skin and his taste buds detect sour syrup. His fingers push into the fruit, as if it were a hollow ball. Unable to decipher now the past greatness of the taste of old, he holds the remnant of destruction in hand.

His labored years of plantation-style farming to produce greatness are now all in vain. Thoughts of failure loom large. Though his irate episode has seized his frame for now, he is truly livid at the nothingness that produced. He gathers himself and walks up to the mothering tree. With a fresh pair of eyes, he reanalyzes the standing structure. A worn-out trunk houses the structure. The limb that produced the fruit he initially ate is the only branch of withered portion on the tree, and the ground is soft and full of moss. Different from the day he fell in love, he shakes his head and starts to walk away.

The owner of the land spots him and heads his way. To the young farmer, conversing about the fruit may help him understand what happened. The aged farmer warrants the talk, giving helpful insight on how he, too, fell for the fruits of a tree. He told the young farmer that nothing is more breathtaking in life than the first encounter they experienced, yet the ground that governs the lands surrounding the tree was stripped dry. The seeds that are planted are from tainted lineage. The tree is to produce one fruit to mesmerize the partaker, yet this tree produced two (one fruit the old farmer ate, and one the young farmer engulfed). The main objective for this tree is to kill the habitat that surrounds the shell, bring the valuable nutrients back, and chemically master one fruit to bear as its offspring.

The tree is in place to steal, rob and destroy. It is cursed with the task to burden the harvest lands. With the land barely rich, the planting of the second tree life produced inedible fruit. The farmers split, having shared the loss of love, having labored and nurtured to only see it not fulfill its end of the anticipated bargaining. The two trees still stand, their roots spread and intertwined to make one. They are forever conjoined until their life cycle is done. The farmers ploy around the lands, looking for reason to cut down the trees--only to realize that to kill them would mean burying the thing that brought them sweet love and joy.

Unevenly Yoked

Understand, you're unevenly yoked. Unified worldly, but spiritually separate, dwelling on different plains. One vessel is supposedly fighting a holy war; the other, a missionary of cult beliefs without any testimony to recite because of a closed soul. She holds him dear, spreading her legs like the wings of an eagle, gracing the atmosphere of relationship woes. Insertion causes a birth of a loving seed with split chromosomes from both settling parents. The morals and foundation are tainted, misguided and built with blasphemy. She thought her mate would change, yet the stubborn genes that lived within him all his days are purely wicked. Sinisterly longing for a union to procreate, festering on an able body to release a spawn into this deceitful world.

Curse the union that was created by unrighteous steps, but even the Lord watches over kids of incongruous behavioral parents. She loves him, even stayed with him when he denounced the Lord Jesus Christ. Still she tried to lay the material of a foundation with carnal rubbish, and the devil helped as he presented her with shelter on sinking sand. The Lord's shepherd emphatically said, "No!" to joining you two in matrimony, so you opted for a false prophet to consolidate the out-of-order relation. You lost yourself, like a prostitute on the dark streets! You allowed the deceitful lies to pump your faith away, like a leech bankrupting your body in hunt for the Lamb's blood.

You never confessed your faith aloud, never asked for mercy or forgiveness. Yet somehow, Jesus saw fit to rescue you once the merger plummeted into oblivion and documents eliminated the alliance. Then, what did you do? Instead of taking time to get close to the mercy of Christ, you freely roamed in the same world from which you were saved. You wore a smile, but also the same burdens that were never placed in Christ's hands. That weight of wants became false needs; backsliding slid you back into the arms of that familiar minion. I pray the bloodsucker that latched onto your vessel left the covering of the Lamb around your soul. I condemn you not, for who am I to judge? Once friends, I now bury that in Mariana Trench as you beget with an unimportant marauder.

Thinking to Myself

I don't chase her like I did the others that left in the past. Don't call her to hear her voice. No crying or begging for mercy. I gave her all I had, along with the part of me that was never given to anyone else. She got everything anyone wanted during her time, and what did I get? A crushed heart, along with a soul stripped of its essence. So now, I replace her with nothing; kill the dream of forever off and wake up to a reality that never showed her uncanny essence at all. The bed we laid in has ownership, the house as well. To live fully resides in me now. Damn whoever doesn't understand that statement!

Your heart can go out to her. I hope whatever is holding her keeps her worldly shell. May the grip of reality continue to strangle stupidity into her throat, cutting off her air passage eventually. As she stays planted, may the ground she walks on sink, like the pit of my heart. As she thinks she finds love again, may the reality of all things left behind run over her vessel, like a Mack® truck going 95 mph and hitting an armadillo on a dark, two-lane highway.

As for me, I can't and won't sit still! I have goals and accomplishments to reach. People will know through testimonial readings the burning desire I have focused in on to make destiny happen. The Lord is my witness in making me a spearhead, hovering through the air as I line up with the target of deliverance. The smile I release radiates my believers. But, for nonbelievers and naysayers, it introduces the uncontrollable feeling of the capital vices. As long as I have breath in my lungs, one had better understand that losing isn't an alternative. I wash my hands in water, which soothes the lines in my palms from the stress caused. Looking at her with love for the old corpse that once enchanted my soul, I oblige the feelings. If a rekindling were ever presented, she would have to work harder than a slave picking cotton with no hands did!

My issues have been addressed and mailed. If the intended receiver never gets the message, then shame on her for changing her address.

The Devil Wore Designer

The devil wore designer, and I purchased the wardrobe. I saw beauty and fell in love. Where I thought I was transforming, I was allowing strength for devilish growth to take place. Places I thought should be seen and shown, yet damned to the world for ages; I only showed what was already seen. So precious and innocent was the latter portion of the duration. Angelic in her bare form, breathtaking to be in the presence of this beast. I became mesmerized in the ambiance that we shared. Nothing more amazing than sharing the same space as something, someone, you truly love.

The devil wore designer, yet only designer from the proceeds of my funds. She consumed the high fashion of the runway as she skated and sashayed her way down streets, hallways and corridors. Arm bent as the handbag rested on the crease between her forearm and bicep. Pose for the camera; her smile is radiant and precise to highlight her bone structure. Conversation adaptive, the ability to morph, win friends and influence people, left all inside a spell. The way the room focused on the outfits, accessories and her figure was astonishing. While I stayed on her opposite arm, the spotlight too transferred to me.

The devil wore designer. Eyewear covered the red pupils as the sun burned down on her brow. Her chariot, British in origin, navigated her through the countryside in a prestigious manner. Mainly chauffeured as the passenger seat nestled her corpse she invaded, staring at bystanders as she rode past them on her travels. Hair blowing in the wind, the breeze separated the strands of each follicle to evenly flow. She worked the sexual areas of her domain, like a soft provocative slow dance with a man in a chair seated for arousal.

The devil wore designer, wore it all in the belief that designer made the world stop and stare. She wore designer, as though it was form fitted to every square inch of the covering she was created with. She played more into the nameplate of others to paste on herself than the nameplate of herself, striking conversation with name-dropping designers like she communicated with them daily. I witnessed the conversion, and though loved, I saw that there was a stronger hold. She was anointed with evil and the spell wore off on me. See the devil wore designer; yet, I did, too. The devil wore designer, killing the saint inside as the evil ensued.

Prisoner of War

The ides of the month are heavy; they are swarming moment after moment. The locus of effects spiral my life into an abyss darker than residency on the arctic ice sheets. I'm remotely positioned with a shell, minus an understanding soul. These problems I hold are my responsibilities; it's my life and my fate. The path I walked has no stumbling blocks or roadblocks; more like a dead end with a cliff that warrants a drop from a distant nebular to earth's shallow ground. The free-falling momentum of my endeavors has me up, lacking sleep. The dates on the calendar mean nothing. The clock hits the same hours as I watch sunrise to sunset multiple times before my red eyes are blanketed by my eyelids.

This can't be right. My heart is golden like the roads of Heaven; yet, I feel like it's asphalt as I get trampled by abusive pedestrians. I want my bed to smother me in its rectangular shape, easing my ailments back to perfect working order. Seems like I hear all the noises of the universe through these ears; thumping sounds that screech a soundtrack to my current days. I need something, something that can take me into a spiritual coma to escape the madness. Acquisitions of me intentionally hurting and harming. Hell, I've been the victim for years. A drunken scheme to break my life into shattering pieces too fine for reconnecting adhesive has me plummeting. The loss of a career I love is hanging on a wet string that is quickly losing its strength as my faith decreases.

I gave too much power; should have confronted this personal problem years ago. Should have bonded one out and locked the other away as the invasion of my records was leaked for their personal gain, minus racketeering. But, what do I do now? I'm screaming at self, not vocally uttering a word. I broke through my breaking point and had enough. Now look at this: charges of insane antics, which even the mentally disturbed think are diabolical. I just want to pray and sleep, sleep and pray. Day after day, I'm constantly reminded. Day after day, I cry my soul's deepest bellow. I need something; the anxiety is becoming too much. Sleep is needed. I'm exhausting my mind. It's reading like psychopathic brain waves when recorded by a therapist. I can remedy the circling thoughts with water and a bottle of sleeping pills.

My eyes are red, along with a heart that is decreasing in warmth. The outside world is moving, while my inside world feels at a halt. One pill, two pills, and then I lose count--on purpose. I wonder if this will really help my cause to find rest from existence. I sway in my nestled position as I dream of genies to allow me three wishes. They must be working as I smile at nightmares of old. If I should die before I wake, I pray the Lord my soul to take. My eyes close and I wrestle no more. Comfortable in a fetal position, I feel like I'm back in the valley of the unborn, ready to get drafted to a new set of predecessors. Lungs full of air, with a steady heartbeat, my muscles relax. I am finally at peace.

The Next Day

It was really over. I died last night as my head soaked into the pillow. I left love on the side of the road after it collided with my reality. My heart was spewed across the pavement. So many people gawking to see my demise, if I could have stayed sleep, it would have been fine with me.

I dreamed of a better place, free of worry. I was alone and happy. My smile was back as the clouds of lost love were nowhere to be found. I searched for nothing because I was looking for nothing. I was at peace. Then, the sun graced my room. The Lord made way for me to see another day.

So, I woke up wishing the light from the sun was eclipsed, darkened like close eyelids in a black cave. I placed my feet on the floor and shook my head, knowing I had to face myself in the mirror. Deep breaths as I pissed out the liquor and pills that put me into a deep trance the night before.

Washing my hands, I closed my eyes before I saw my reflection. As I opened them, I didn't recognize the image that stared back. Bags under my eyes, lines in my face, I was a shell of my former existence. My facial expressions boiled my soul. I had let love leave and buried my manhood, with no headstone to rest on the plot.

The rage in me grew. She was gone; I understood that. But the lack of fight bothered me. Life was a game to her; I get it. So, from me to her, she would not beat me in life! I was far from being okay, but I was close to being the person she would regret.

I got ready to hit the ground running. My new lease on life never led me to look for her. But sometimes, her life found me. Yet, I was yesterday's memories. The ones left for dead with no oxygen in my lungs. I was blindsided by deceit with a fatal blow of lies.

I wasn't perfect, but I'd be damned if I wasn't perfect to the naked eye. The stories would follow; I get that. The questions would be asked; I understand that. But, looking for her? That would never happen from this point forward.

That same sun that graced my brow gave me hope for better. Dreams still breathed deep in my soul for love. I was given a chance of a lifetime to prove someone else wrong that didn't think I would amount to anything. Those tears I once cried were filled in buckets to water my grass. I wanted her to see how healthy it was on my side of the fence, compared to the barren land that she thought was full of riches.

So, tonight, I burn the bed we once slept on. The sheets, pillows, and all things left behind will be the fuel till the ashes give way. And when I wake tomorrow, all the things that I was unable to do will now be done. If daddy was a rolling stone, his son will be the successor to his throne.

The Call of the Wild

I was out of my element. I was a free man in a world full of vultures circling me, like prey taking its last breath. I had a new lease on life, with no shackles holding me down to one woman. I didn't answer to anyone, had no one in my life to speak for me on this dating scene. I slithered streets like a lion in the brush, tall grass researching my kill as I prepared to pounce atop of her. Kill after kill, there were too many animals in my jungle to stay confined to one genotype.

Sweet nothings I whispered in their ears, easing their hesitations with reassurance that they didn't have to go any further. They trusted me with their treasure chests, and each Pandora Box I opened of these women led me to trap my evils inside them. I sealed their wombs with tarnished remnants of my blind eye, searching during this consented robbery. The way they scratched for more. Erotic to me, the way they bit their bottom lips. I took pride in hearing the moans of my name from lips I barely kissed. I was an animal without a home. I was the king of all I survey. Little did any woman know the power of prison I put their body as they wrestled with open legs and pores.

I roamed, looking not for my next attack. But, I merely found the touch that wasn't in my life anymore. I felt the skin of queens with no crown trying to locate completion between horizontal lips. I kissed until the voices said, "Enough!" as their bodies danced alone in a bed with beautiful seizures from taste buds tingling on their spot. I stared down on them, with my vision focused on the demolition of walls—not by the men who hurt them—but more of expanding the ones that tightened the canal they worked hard to keep intact.

I was caught up in my shallowness of being alone, and they were weak in the knees of enjoying my pain as pleasure. If the eyes told what my heart wanted to say, they would've never gave me the okay to pierce their packages. Yet, they did, and I sucked the air out until released. I gently laid them to rest, with a closed casket harboring a part of me forever.

The streets weren't one-sided. They knew the baggage I brought along with me. I was infatuated with the opportunity to roller coast on a ride for free. They jumped the line in my amusement park and test rode all of me they could handle until the park closed. Free entrance each day, although the dresser grabbed money like a child's piggybank.

They let themselves out as I stared at ceiling fans counting revolutions of the blades. Where was love? Why was it eluding me during my most vulnerable time? I made love to strangers like they had committed eternity of earth to me. At the rate I was going, my bank account would be empty from depositing myself into many institutions before I found the right one. I lived like women were meat, and I needed to devour quantity instead of savoring the opportunity to cultivate one dish forever.

But, I wasn't ready to give in. I wasn't ready to let go of this feeling of control. I owned high self-esteem when with them. Little did I know, it came with low morals and misguided pathways. I was almost my own voice of self-righteousness, until my phone rang from the one girl I never had the opportunity to tell my true feelings to. "Don't put off what you can do today," they taught me. So once more, I listened to her pains, and then softly whispered sweet nothings in her ear. She invited me over to her place as the horizons placed hues over my Serengeti. She was the prettiest gazelle in the jungle, yet tonight, she didn't run. She literally laid there and let me deflower every inch of her as I pollinated her lotus flower.

Midnight Marauder

She was that piece of the past I admired and adorned. She possessed my wants and needs, but timing never saw fit. We defied our realities and backstroked in lust hundreds of times while in relationships with others. We fell in love with infatuation first, then formed our union in lust.

I dreamt of this succubus before she ever slept with me. The way she lured her way into my dreams, seducing me in a way that I searched for more. She was crafty in her positioning, providing me with enough to call her name and curse the walls that enclosed our activities. Yet, she played with my key in her locked treasure chest, until she felt like unlocking the watery confinement of jewels.

She's forever my forbidden fruit in the garden of no sin of which I rebelliously bit. The way her nectar graced my taste buds as she tried to communicate phrases. I learned to tame this demon. I learned to control her sinister attitude and pillage her village until she submitted to my control. I became fluent in her body's language, French kissing both lips till both tongues spoke in shivering dialect.

My goal was to be *with* her. I wanted the words she uttered to be true. I needed her nails to rake my back and chest as she lost control of mind, body and soul all at once. I needed to steal her away like she did nightly to me. Whomever she laid next to needed not possess her anymore. My bed awaited her. My key fit her lock and we twisted in every combination to make sure we were compatible.

I was out of my relationship, free from the shackles that made me creep around in the brisk winds of the night. No hotels or secret messages needed to jar me away to lust in her womb. I'm ready for reality to know my secret dream. Dangerously, I needed to purge her pores feverishly fornicate our frustrations. I needed to couple that with her sitting atop my Eiffel Tower as she beat my chest like King Kong nightly.

I wanted to be more than just her incubus. I needed her—and more than a relationship predicated on the transference of bodily fluids. I wanted our name on the house and to receive mail together, not just the graffiti I sprayed on the walls of her uterus. I wanted time to be on my side for once. In love, I lust for her, and time only granted me the opportunity to lust for her love. So I sleep alone as she lays next to a man that only dives into her ocean, but doesn't unlock the treasures in her abyss. I wonder if she talks to the moon, like I do on those sleepless nights when I howl for her touch.

Magnetic Infatuation

We were two givers, magnets that latched onto each other's body like polyurethane adhesive. We caressed, painted and stretched each other's canvas. We were artists, each of us leaving images on the other's mind. Our work stayed on full display, but our erotic museum stayed closed off to the public for viewing.

The admission was free, yet the way she fit in her clothes would entice me to pay her way. Her body was sculpted and brushed with gold leaf. The way she peeled the fabric off her frame made me jealous of the material that got to touch her all day. I was an admirer of beauty, and she was gorgeous in every manner.

She was electricity, a surge of goodness that powered my carnal station. When we connected, our heat melted the core within a power plant. Our reactors toppled the scale of safety when combined. The way our meters redlined, neighboring residents and animals needed evacuation for safety. We always started out as a tropical depression, with upgrades into a tropical storm.

The way the sheets absorbed our sweat and fluids left a tantalizing crime scene under black light review. The comforter would canopy my body as I snaked into her secret garden. The pillows became teething toys, or muzzles for loud moans. Though it was daylight in the room, her headlights stayed on and hard, like blood in the spear of her warrior.

She was prey on my empty stomach of lust. Her appetite for me was that of a malnourished human at a buffet. Our menu was served in many combinations. No matter the time, swallowing and a full belly was a given.

We toasted our thirst with a rare bottle from '69. The finest nectar against the taste buds at the back of the palate for satisfaction. We pinned each other down, like wrestlers in a ring, with each match ending in a draw or victory by the smallest margin. A rematch right after the refractory period.

We kissed and necked, brought sexual relation to a head before penetration paved the way. Her body had a scent that blanketed my lungs with her superpowers. The way she parked her lips on my abdominal muscles, kissing and sliding down gently, she parted her chest with my private eye. Tricks with her tongue left me speechless as the hair left outside the ponytail swept my hip flexor.

Fingerprints on the walls and ceilings, DNA under her nails, she rested with my handprints on her backside. With clothing in obscure places, we left our mark on the territory. Laying down or standing up—didn't matter. The bed, floor or shower left no sections of the imagination untamed. We were a Category 5 hurricane, with catastrophic results. At the end of the continuum, we were merely megawatts of satisfaction to each other. A pleasurable infatuation with chart setting activities.

Breakfast

The morning sun illuminates on the windowpane. The rays grace the skin of a couple bound in love. Lust brings the two into one another's arms, yet the aura of each other's presence casts a spell that cupid's arrow of love couldn't cast.

Hugged tightly in the arms of her lover, she slightly rubs her head in the creases of his chest. She rests on his right bicep, as if it was a pillow plush with the softest down feathers. Her leg warms his legs. He lies on his back as she sleeps on her side. The two fit like a glove, handcrafted to perfection.

The sun warms her skin. She slowly opens her eyes to invite the morning presence into her grace. As her vision comes to, she stares at the individual that gave her a night full of passion and exhilaration, unmatched by anyone else.

She moves gently, only to awaken him as she tries to crawl out the bed. He instantly says, "Good morning, baby," and plants a passionate forehead kiss on her.

She responds, "Good morning, sunshine," and smiles to show how good it feels in his arms. They gaze at each other, only to understand the amount of love that connects the two.

She breaks the silence by trying to roll out the bed. As she places her feet on the ground, he snatches her back in his arms and says, "Please don't leave me."

She laughs and promptly says, "I'll be right back."

She leaves the room, and he watches as she sashays away. In love with her structure, he employs eagle-eye concentration, lusting as he counts her steps that make her butt jiggles seductively. He rolls back over and grabs the pillow that once covered her nestled frame. He swallows her scent and falls back asleep in love.

She finds refuge in the kitchen. Sitting down at the kitchen table, still feeling her legs shaking from the night prior, she crosses her legs. But the vibration of her legs shaking moves the table centerpiece. She grabs hold to the idea of cooking breakfast for her worthy love partner.

With nothing on, but a skin tight t-shirt and a pair of seductive panties, she warrants her plan of action. She preheated the stove and rambled through the cabinets, making sure there was enough variety to fill the stomachs for both of their frames.

As the aroma crept through the house, the smell tickled the nose of her lover. He promptly awakens to the smell of sweet cooking from his goddess. He sat up, only to decipher each entrée. As the visuals entered his mind, he rolled out the bed to accompany her as she cooked.

Naked in stance, he grabbed a pair of shorts and walked through the house shirtless. He stood in the threshold of the kitchen doorway, admiring the view he had of her legs spread apart--with posture firmly committed to cooking over a hot stove. His mind raced as he stared. He loves the gap between her legs. The way her derrière overlapped the panties that she wore. The tight t-shirt that snuggled her torso. It was a combination of elements, but he was in agreement that they were all in the right spot.

Unaware of his presence, he snuck up behind her. He simultaneously placed his left hand on her side and kissed the back of her neck. She jumped, as if someone was breaking into the house. But violation wasn't happening. She accepted the gesture.

He thanked her for the preparation of the meal, telling her that it wasn't necessary. She referred to it as a "thank you" for the night prior. The way he gave to her was like never before. Though they had encountered one another before, she wanted to show her appreciation.

They stood in the kitchen, with him standing behind her, gripping her tightly. She smiled, letting him know the embrace of his arms was enough to make her melt from his love.

She walked away to retrieve plates from the cabinets. He stood watching, biting his bottom lip, as she walked away. As she turned, she noticed his stance, as well as the look in his eyes. It turned her on, but she didn't want to attack him from the lust that had now come over her.

She proceeded to walk past him. He immediately stopped her by putting his hand out to grab her. She smiled as the two looked like they wanted to attack one another. She stopped the occurrence by twisting out his arms and placing the plates on the table. He approached her, only to be stopped by her telling him she needed to put the biscuits in the oven.

She walked to the fridge to locate the item as he looked on in amazement. As she walked to the counter to place them on a tray, he once again grabbed her. This time, turning her toward him. She smiles as he lowers her head to kiss her on her lips. The can of biscuits falls to the ground.

Her fingers run through his hair, as his hands move in both a north and south direction. His left hand massages her back as he eases his way up. His right hand migrates down her spinal cord to grab a handful of her bottom, lifting her on her toes.

The two wrestle with each other in an erotic manner, showing the passion they contain when connected in touch. Lust and love quarrel between which one is superior. As minutes pass, lust wins the argument.

Her nipples harden as the sign of lovemaking enters the room. He pulls her shirt over her head, exposing her torso. His head lowers as he takes a mouth full of breast and caresses it with his tongue. His loose hand now massages the unoccupied breast. He slightly runs his teeth over the nipple, giving her a tingle down her spine. She releases her juices as her panties catch them like a sponge. She feels his mid-section poking against her body, but she wants to feel all of him inside of her.

He slowly lowers his left hand. Taking his fingers, he lowers one side of her panties. Once they reach the furthest point, he does the same with the right side of the article. She raises her legs individually to drop the panties to the floor.

As he maneuvers her garments, she too makes advances in the sexual department. She unties his shorts, causing them to drop to the floor and expose his nudity. He moves his legs to kick the shorts away from his personal area. She kisses his neck, using excessive tongue and lips.

He grabs both sides of her behind and grips it, with no intention of releasing. The grip spreads the inner lips of her vagina, allowing the juices to drip freely. He lifts her off her feet where she is now elevated eight feet high. He lowers her, only to strategically place her on top of the counter.

She opens her eyes, only to find him lowering his body to one knee. His head forces her to spread her legs further. She tries to grab him to pull him up, but it's too late. The lock of his parallel lips to her vertical ones has engaged. He opens his mouth and releases his tongue. He locates her clitoris and wiggles it to stimulate her past her breaking point.

Her back arches as her head rests against the cabinets. She shakes as he searches her treasure for jewels. Deep breaths accompanied by jerking from her torso now have her speaking in an un-mastered dialect. She curses as she continues to release her taste into his mouth.

He rises up, kissing her on her neck. He lifts her in the air—this time, slowly lowering her onto his mid-section. Piercing her lips, penetration has occurred. He lowers her in the slowest and most careful manner ever imagined. She wraps her arms around his neck and draws her head closer to kiss his ear. She bites her lips and scratches his back as he bounces her up and down.

She tries to pull back, a reaction from the erotic nature they are sharing. Her breasts bounce in a circular motion as she accepts the pleasure. He notices her muscles fatiguing, so he finds a free spot on table. He gently walks her over, as she swears he is hitting her cervix wall.

He places her down gently as she looks in amazement. He licks between her legs several more times to lubricate her area. She falls back into pleasure. He pulls her legs around his torso and places himself back inside her. She arches her back again and feels every part of him. In-and-out movements have her throwing dishes on the floor. Luckily, the cooked food remains on the stove.

As he goes deeper, she belts out loud curse words and screams his name. Several times, she climaxed, with several more to come. She lies flat, only to have a tear drop fall from her eye.

She is in love and he, too. The two make music that has nature watchers jealous of the chords they hit. Angelic passes of sexual acts has conception jealous. They are meant for one another. Time is still to allow them grace and mercy.

Almost an hour into the act, he climaxes. She feels it shoot into her, like a bullet. Both exhausted, they are thankful for the union. Respect is mutual, and they know they were born for one another.

He walks out and heads to the bathroom, as she lays there for a minute. He comes back, picks her up, and carries her to a warm bubble bath. Together, they soak. She rests her head and falls into a slumber. He washes her gently and she accepts the offer.

They realize the act was great, but at the expense of an uneaten breakfast. They understand though that when love is in your heart, everything else can wait!

The Clouded Mind

The smoke rises to the ceiling, my head pressed against the couch, as I exhale the smoke. My hand grips the glass. Two ice cubes submerge in the liquor as I drown my sorrows. My shirt is off, tattoos exposed to breathe the pain my body has endured. My feet are propped up on the coffee table, just inches away from the half pint and sticky cabbage.

I'm drifting on my memories, with Al Green playing in the backdrop of my radio. The room is moving as the light from the lamp leaves shadows on my walls. I'm high! I'm gone in a sense that reality looks different through these bloodshot eyes. My heart is jumping out of my chest! The thumps beat a drum pattern that awakens my soul.

I'm confused and searching for answers. I'm sitting still and listening to irrational emotions, alone in a home, but together in connection. I'm connected to two, which makes the number one. One big triangle of love and lust. Can love be divided equally between three individuals, and they love me for who I am? Can time allow me the opportunity to give enough of myself to both hearts, and yet hurt no one?

I'm tripping! The glass raises as the liquor burns my throat. I'm exhausted in thoughts, but the memories are so fond. The times were great, and neither one has ever let me down. Am I selfish to want them both? Life isn't easy, but it is slightly great to have an option when you want to be with someone—and not the one that pissed you off. They both complete me, whether for an hour or the whole night. They are different entirely. Their makeup and attitudes are nothing alike at all.

Deep coughs hurt my lungs; the strains cause my eyes to water. I babble my speech, as if someone is in the room listening. I'm flipping through photos in my phone, trying to get a glimpse of perfection. I'm measuring their curves with my eyes, smiling at the nakedness of their shells. I'm not comparing, but one has a little more of that than the other, and vice versa. This is weird! The liquor and weed mix has these pictures dancing in front of me. I should've at least recorded us having sex. That would have been so perfect right now.

The way their bodies infused with mine screamed perfection. I just want to love on one, emotionally attach to her mind. Take my lips and kiss her earlobe as I sing a soulful song. I want their thoughts to be under attack, forever reminiscing like my thoughts are right now. What if they never care about the negativity of this world? I'm an opportunist, an opportunist with lurking ambition to caress their soul. I never wanted them both at the same time—just undivided attention during excavation in their watery grave as I probed.

But, the world started talking. The onslaught of questions revealed their faces to each other. They knew each other's names, maybe even knew the time was split between them. Phone calls and angry messages, they cursed the life that I lived for their humiliation. Somewhere in me, I loved them both and wanted to make it right, but how? I was banned and outlawed, unable to liberate any positive thoughts of me back into their minds. They were forever linked because of my promiscuous lifestyle.

The cloud of smoke married the black cloud I had hovering over me. Liquor and regret caused thunder and lightning to water my cheeks. I sat in my sorrows, drunk and high, with remorse for what I did to them. Maybe one day, they will understand that I was truly in love with both of them, just uncommitted to either. I'll look for happiness in this bottle of corn whiskey because sunshine isn't walking through my bedroom door tonight.

I hear the clicking of the clocks on the wall. Each second that tick tocks causes me to blink my eyes to focus. My mind projects mirages at the foot of the bed. The illustrations of a perfect woman dances above me as my tired body fights sleep. The revolutions in the ceiling fan breezes a scent into my lungs. I lean up to see who has forgiven me, as the light from the fan shadows their face. I reach to grab her by the waist, smiling at the way the definition in her legs entices me at the moment. As she bends down, I tell her, "I love you." Before I can touch, she disappears. I'm hallucinating. I feel the bond to the purgatory confines I locked myself into as I stretch for the intimate touch of the women I forfeited in my life.

Making Love to Loveless Shells

I was alone in love with the notion of love. Oh, how I wanted love's scent within my sheets; her warm body on the other side of the pillow. I'm daydreaming of love's touch caressing my frame and erotically satisfying my lonely needs.

Introductions and small talks cause my essence to breathe air into various ladies' lungs. They engulf my dialect as I swoon them into curiosity, making their mind tornado while their grail hurricanes. I maintain my ego, but my mouth adds gasoline into our hot scenery. My lips kiss fare maidens, interlocking their tongues around mine as I lay them delicately on their backs. They looked with seductive eyes as I unbuttoned their blouses. Bit bottom lips as I unstrapped bras. They uttered, "What are you doing?" as I pulled panties and pants past their ankles simultaneously. I ran my tongue over goosebumps, spelling *LUST* from their navels to their breasts. I massaged their backs and kissed centimeters from their vertical gateways. In one sweeping motion, I maneuvered to their necks, piercing my entry and anchoring their relaxed bodies with a boat anchor that could stop the Titanic before it hit the iceberg. They gripped my skin as I inched inside canals; I became an explorer of beautiful women's holiness.

Open mouths with deep sighs. Spiritual women cursed the heavens as the ceiling faded when their eyes rolled to the backs of their heads. Legs opened wider than the pores that sweat from friction. The ones that called names called names; they told me a body that didn't belong to me was now all mine. The cocky ones, who claimed they didn't scream, screamed and panted when sections of their insides never touched before by grace were inhabited.

I lay on my back, allowing them to feel like they had an opportunity to last while straddling my saddle. They eased their knees down by my ribs, placed their hands in the crease of my chest, and rode like a bucking horse trying to unseat the rider. Within minutes, the backs of their necks were ringing wet as they rolled their hips--the inability to control their bodies from ecstasy shaking once their pelvis popped.

They released their needs several times in one sitting. They held tight to my frame with exhausted corpses, but I was detached. They wanted to cuddle and sleep; I simply wanted my space and alone time. Then, one day, I realized the issue wasn't them, but me. I made love to those that were only in my company for sex. Now I must live with pieces of my soul sprinkled in various grails as I searched for love's *love*. How can one be complete when he is a jigsaw of fragments embedded on stained walls, like thrown paint clashing with the interior décor of the women that now lust for him?

Abstaining

I have been celibate for four days, six hours and 52 minutes. I know it's mind over matter, but I'm thinking with a mind that has no brain waves. The blood is rushing like Niagara Falls, but blocked like it's a dam made by beavers and man. I'm trying to protect my heart and soul from the jezebels that suck my impurities dry, yet the drug is calling my name. I am far from an addict, so let's call me a fully functional member of denial.

It's something about the skin of a woman than warms my frame. The sight of her eyes rolling as her speech misplaces words in her sentence. How the conversation goes from words to moans. How her limbs relax and believe in my attitude to learn her love language. The way her voice becomes the stroke my ego needs to please her every desiring moment.

I'm looking for more than the encounters of casual pleasure. I'm searching for long-term gratification from a woman that doesn't want to share my blessing with another. A woman whose lips ignite a fire in my loins that can set a forest fire in the winter months. The curves on her frame will allow my hands to roller coast as I massage the temple that I cherish. I need her to have all the attributes of flesh, as well as the spiritual understanding that the heavens connected us. I need one woman, with one set of breasts, one derriere, child-bearing hips, and a will to give and receive.

It's been four days, seven hours and too many minutes since I've been abstaining. The last time I made love to someone that I wasn't in love with, she looked at me in disbelief that her pocketbook could be filled. Her inner walls watered colors as I removed my strong arm from her hold. She panted in cold sweat, as her pores opened from the encounter with ecstasy. She stared in disbelief, and I looked on in confusion. Her body never reacted like that. Never had her mouth wanted to say, "Enough!" when her body gave more. Never had her soul detached from her body and watched her shell limberly gyrate as a man wrote a love letter inside her. I had one chance to get it right. That, I did—but it scared her senseless.

I guess I still made love like I was in my last relationship. A few unworthy patrons that left no money on my dresser for the rollercoaster ride of their life. I never dumb down my activity to offset the fact they don't see their own worth. I needed alone time. I needed time to sit still and figure out me, without damaging another woman's womb with gratification of being able to open her treasure box and ferment the air with her lotus flower.

It's been too many days, a lot of hours, and more minutes than I care to count. I am looking for a queen. So heavy is the head that wears the crown. Maybe one day, heavy will be the finger that wears my diamond as my queen.

Conflict of Heart

I'm battling the various sounds my myogenic muscular organ is making, several renditions of symphonies to thrashing chords of the intro and outro of horror movies. The plagued mind of successful thoughts fights the warfare of the world's deceitfulness. Many days, I thought the beeping was faint and weary, too weary for me to showcase love. Vague thumps were felt when I placed my right palm on my chest; yet, I knew it was more to me than this.

I've loved, but love hasn't been pouring into me one drop of Cupid's venom from his soaked arrows. I've given my all, prayed for strength to conquer more days standing alongside a mate irrelevant to my forthcoming. Yet, there is distance. The side-by-side feels like I'm ahead with maturity, yet reaching back with more than a helping hand for their advancement. I've been holding my opposite hand out, hoping they would take it and walk with me through life; yet, I stand alone. I'm staring at their back; they constantly look inverted at the past immaturity they can't let go. My future has no reverse, so I can't indulge in looking in a rearview mirror for hope.

I stand concrete to love, but the long days give me a shadow that is gaining in size. My earth is tilting in faith, and my shadow looks like it's running away from my body. These weary heartbeats have me wondering about my mental health. My psyche is fatigued at times; I'm lying down, resting, as I await my heart to be found. I gave it away; no telling if the person who has it is cherishing it or has pawned it on the black market in earth's doom. The behavior they are depicting is not that of a relationship. I'm ready for another chapter in life. I have dreams that are destined to perform in my reality. My prayers need to reach the throne. I need a message to be funneled into my soul. I need the guidance of spiritual navigation to lead me away from the turmoil brush that is indigenous to my relational habitat.

Lord, rest my corpse. Find fit in my slumber to form me a helpmeet. Lord, make me anew so I can be that person for someone else equally. I'm tired, but not weak; I'm going through so you can craft what will be my testimony. My heart is faint; you have strengthened it as I've grown closer. It beats louder with understanding of your voice; my soul is about to run over. I yell not to the heavens anymore, for you stand next to me as you hear my heart's desire. Love isn't enough to show you my faithfulness. Why would I accept just that from others?

My extended palm still levitates, and my significant other still hasn't grabbed hold of my indication. Lord, walk with me down governed paths and lead me into thine blessings. Cover me with favor. Shield me with amour as I use my speech to deliver anointed passages. My heart is conflicted. I am a child of the King, roaming amongst lurking minions. Restore my heartbeat to a vibrant thump. Send me a mate who I can dance a choreographed waltz with in the rain from angels' tears falling from Heaven.

Shake up my world. Filter the trash of the land, and deliver a mate that will bathe in the cup of your love, allowing our union to pour out blessings. Baptize us in your eyes. Allow the world to bask in the love we will have in our sight. Rest my weary heart to prepare me. Complete me in you so I can be awarded a complete mate. I thank you for this storm, this conversation, and deliverance, Lord. My shell feels fatigued. Thank you for the interior renovation that is about to transform me.

Lord, Please Keep Me

Lord knows I've tried, sacrificed dreams with time to allow a connection with love. I've removed some entities, those needed and those that barely made sense. I almost lost myself; yet, some of the people peeking into my world think I'm already there. I love *love,* and the completion of a union lies in the Lord. Lord, I lay my prayers at your feet. I couldn't send this delivery by an angel because it was just that precious to me. I'm on my knees, arms extended with my head in my shoulders. My tears sparkle on the golden throne. I need you now!

The streets seem one-sided. The direction is right, yet the journey's scenery isn't conducive to my picture reel. The memories are great, fun times with invigorating stories that light up the sky. The world is theirs, though I've traveled these roads. We dwell in the same universe. The understanding of this possession baffles people. How are they to comprehend when they can't register love? It seems so promising. I claimed this relationship before I uttered, "I love you" to *love.*

I longed for her, carried myself with debonair charisma that migrated a room to my presence. I released myself, spread my ashes of old self, like a cremated vessel on the streets of my city. Lord, you found me, every last dust particle that blew in the wind. You made me anew, formed a new man, and breathed new life into my vessel. So, I came back to you. With thanksgiving and hope, I placed my dreams at your feet. I'm unworthy of this, yet you saw fit to plant love in my soul. My spirit sends blessings to you, for a wretch like me was given a gift from God. My body carries your image. The mirror shows me a figure, but my reflection amongst your children commands your righteousness.

Each life is a season. Lord, whatever you're doing, please don't do it without me. Whatever you see fit for me, I proudly accept it and testify on it. I've been lost before, stuck my hands out and felt for objects. I then calmed down, remembered your voice, and asked for sight. You placed so much on me; therefore, my load is manufactured by you. Since you know my makeup, Lord, dump the fittings of righteousness on me so I can be a mighty man in Christ. I'm blessed to have you as a Father. Thank you for seeing fit to create me and mold me, bringing me out of this womb many call a world.

Dear God, If You're Listening…

I feel my right foot tapping like the foot peg of a drum set, slowly beating the bass drum, like the thumping within my heart. A light tapping on the riding cymbal as it is hit on the bow, along with soft key strokes from a Yamaha piano rotates the room I'm in. The melody has me shaking my head slowly with collapsed eyes. Underneath my eyelids are tears, finding outlets to run on, showcasing a drained heart. My skin lumps up like concrete streets paved with rocks. The chills bring a reaction of warmth to my soul as I sniffle once. Raising my head while swaying it back and forth, I open my eyes to connected lashes bonded together from frustration.

My lips tremble as I begin to speak. Empty room at first sight, yet I know I am not alone. I own the voice of a child, for my Father knows and hears my cry. I have walked as far as I can go. I've lost navigation along with self. Today, I give up on wondering. Father, I used to love, found unconditional during a time in life where all was corrupt. My heart beats smoothly with a chilled flow of blood. I'm stagnant in the stride of dreams; my reality is obsolete from wants. I'm touching places within others' hearts that no man has ever been able to go. So, I stay away from mental games that might break their psyche if relations don't grow. Lord, you know my desires for a family. My uncontrolled substance of overflowing love trickles blessings through the DNA released to the production of these wants.

My yearning for healthy children who are vibrant, with carefree emotions that light the darkest sky, allowing my frustration within days to be voided as I leave ill rebuke on the doorsteps of my love. The ability of provisions with the only time needed is present within those confines of falsified want. Father, I come with a bowed head and humble heart. Lord, I tried walking alone on a road that you created through the breath you breathed into my lungs. I'm eternally grateful for this day and the life I've been awarded. Yet, today is the day when my body stands still. My future is now blurred and the past has molded me.

Dear God, if you're listening, the life you have created has a way of humbling one down. Looking over my shoulders, there isn't anything. I come to you with outreached hands, asking for you to lead me, asking for you to engulf my soul and protect it. Previous steps release images, times of obedience and unguided choices. Yet, this next step, I need to walk with you forever. I give myself to you for the desires of my future. Lord, if you're listening, show me a star in the sky that I can see during the height of a sunny day. Let her image be breathtaking, like releasing my soul in my final moments of life. Let me fall to the ground, as if I am a limp corpse looking into the eyes of an angel. Allow her kiss to breathe new life into me every time the tissues of our lips touch.

Father, I am dropping to my knees on this road of frustration and deceit. My tears have formed a moat around me, drowning my former self. Dear God, if you're listening, baptize me and bring me anew in these high waters. Ready for the insertion of so much, you are the holder of true deliverance. The instruments of background melody bond together as the chords release the worship of faith into the air. The room is covered and I am inside imprisonment of His Holy Spirit. Anew, I am, with cleansed frame to release my soul to someone to accept God's gift, when delivered. I am walking with you, Lord, down this road; for I know you will intersect the right street soon. Two intersections, but one house, one family nestled in love. A covenant approved through one of your shepherds, with children christened inside your holy house. Dear God, I know you're listening because I know and hear your voice when you speak back!

Indefinite Angel of Mine

My mind has me seeing you. The dreams of mine have me wondering for you. Your face is translucent to my vision; the smile of yours is lifted by facial muscles and cheekbones. I have been in the company of your personality. It has blown me away with your trait to spotlight your aura. A commanding figure has inanimate objects, fighting for the opportunity to touch your fame. Your skin is soft to the touch. It sparkles and shines, like an angel emerging from a short swim, allowing the sun to glisten off the water. Unafraid to get your hair wet, the moisture curls the follicles into another style, inviting your versatility into the equation. Those piercing eyes of yours have me emerged into your soulful thoughts, giving me the entrance into your world of thinking.

I see your goals, your dreams, your wants. I understand your move as time is spent getting to know you. You house a strong will to love, releasing your emotional realms to give your heart and trust to me as your special someone. I want to love, to give myself to you as we prepare for life as one. One family, one heart, one love connected spiritually by our one high God. From God, you will be given, through my faith and obedience. As I see you, my mind says to call your name as you enter my presence. Yet, I know not your name because it hasn't been released from the heavens. So we shall periodically converse through a transversal tied in spiritually, trickling along key things that shows our connection that will be covenanted. Enjoy life alone for now, as I shall do the same. Any given moment, I can find you in my thoughts and me in yours. I'm waiting for the day we form an intersection of four perfect right angles. Your thinking is like mine. This intersection bears a cross of our faith; it will finally deliver us to each other at the perfect time in life. My wandering rib will be found, giving completion to God's puzzle of man and woman.

Enigmatic Company to Them

What is it? Is the company I give off to them, the company they want to keep forever? Things started with no strings attached. Now, if I need space to breathe, they want to make sure it's not polluted first. So they breathe my atmosphere to inhale the scent of love within a man with a heart that's caring and warm. Yet, the invasion has me backing away at a rapid pace because they weren't looking for me; their definition of love was dead to them. Never would they get the total package within a man without compromise of who they are; yet, prayers do come true. However, one must be ready once they are delivered.

They try to understand me, though to do so is to explain, classify, and properly arrange an enigma that one never encountered a day of their life. They want to tap into my soul, unmask the face of the warrior I have been for years. I run not from my past. Truthfully sharing always leaves concern on their hearts about mine. For the understanding of those who want to know, my heart is mine with a bill of sale from God to live on earth with a spiritual covering. I await a rib, whether broken, engulfed in a body cast, or accompanied by a split. It's mine from the deliverance of my prayers. To understand that is to understand the trials of supposed to be love. Their questions are asked and I fabricate not one segment of my life. But to ask a question to a person in order for one to elaborate will allow me to develop sentences that utter abstract designs, which make the listener feels like they've lived within the confines of the fiber interior to the canvas that is wrenching their autonomy.

How do I tame the passion of communication if I am concupiscent about my present that characterized the man from my proceedings? Their futuristic ponderings are simplified when asked. To ask about occurrences that haven't, or will, take place is mundane to me. From this, their heart, soul, and mind grow heavy, while trying to occupy my company. The festering thoughts that create mythological creations incubate their cerebral-like tormented souls, deceased without permanent residency in neither Heaven nor Hell to call home. Whatever it is, it is of me--bonded in my bloodstream and concreted in the strands of my DNA. Who am I to dissect the delicate deliberations of their finds as it relates to their attraction?

The Dreamer

Late night has my mind racing; devilish interaction has my thoughts pacing.

My feet tap the sheet; my eyelids gain strength, but my pupils get weak.

They dilate to the smallest circle to focus on the ceiling with no light.

I listen to jets that fly by, as my real life and imagination fight.

Time isn't on my side, and my eyelids start to slide. I give in for unexpected dreams that seem to be left in my subliminal start, only to awaken and come to life.

Dreams are the figments of one's untamed thoughts, which wrestle with untamed reality.

They interact to form unparalleled intersections. They are short stories of a narrator of unframed fashion. They depict numerous counts of unconscious acts that seem like reality; unforeseen events that are housed in the mental vault that shouldn't ever be released. Thoughts so explicit that the evils resurrect them from being deceased. They play through the mind's projection reel the repercussions of prayers for want. The asking of a new invention into the life of weltering passion causes the dream to release the perfect outing. Dreams intersect the flow of heartaches and insist on showing times of immaculate want. The things that made one toss and turn now have one wrestling with themselves.

There is nothing more invigorating, nothing more exhilarating, than a dream that chronicles one transformation from fiction to reality. Exhausted formations of a conceived interest releases the essence of a dignified partnership that's the reservoir of wanted, but not the correct given affection. Dreams become complex wordplay that is translated into picture perfect harmony. The strings on the guitar are plucked as the keys on the piano are pressed. They massage the eardrums and insinuate a vibrant tone through the ear. Dreams are the chills that shiver the body of the dreamer. Shakes the sweat out of the pores and douses the purest core with a refreshing irrigation.

Dreams are the hidden secrets that the narrator needs to come alive. They are camouflaged in repetitive format that beg for a broken record sequence. Dreams beg for the interaction of new material; creativity feeds the hunger of this beast. Dreams are only as long as the body can stay asleep. They become more fiction than reality as the daylight hits the windowpane. The light irritates the projection of taboo interaction. Just before a finale, the rested eyes wake.

Early morning insinuates a new day, but past nights long for reoccurring dreams, only to recollect the dreamer's wants through thoughts. Alarm clocks ring as one's body transgresses into a journey with new time. And just as bright as the sunshine, the now awakened dreamer tries to reenact the memories that eased the burden of what a touch of

Heaven felt like. They dream during the day, only to be classified as a daydreamer. They wish for night just to see if the thought will stalk them. The cycle becomes a want, and the mission now becomes a burning passion. So they search to find, look to see, but second guess what they want could never be.

Dream on, dreamer. Reality is amongst you.

Right Insides, Wrong Outsides

Sometimes, we arrive at a place in our life that causes us to reconstruct our essence. We are open to new things, in hopes of finding a different sense of tranquility. Sometimes, a stranger can have a clear open lane onto a highway of life with no speed limit. They are merging their vehicle onto the roadways of someone else's property, but they are fully aware that this person's road may lead them to the destination of a relationship with the owner of the byway.

The speed of travel is sometimes moderate, where cruising is the term of choice to describe the pace of the stranger. Others can configure a car without a governor to regulate the speed, and try to speed into the heart and soul of the recipient. The driver is allowed to ride the road by picking up a passenger, the owner of the road, prior to entrance. The allowance from the owner is different. Where he drives classic cars, she loves new-age design. A stretch for her to ride with emissions hazards, but she tries to find the joy in the ride. He captures the perfect road trip through the countryside, running around mountains and around plains that showcase the "blue grass" countryside. She is more receptive to the coastline that illuminates the sunset as the sun departs to night and the transition hits the ocean just right.

The car handles greatly to be so different in its insides, but houses modern-day technology to keep the handling modernized. Yet, the physical characteristics weigh heavy on her heart. The personality is great, but are the outside characteristics really that far out her box that she can't fathom the journey to last longer than the next rest stop? The driver feels he is all she wants. He revs the motor from time to time, flaunting the loud rumble of his motor. The passenger sits and stares out the window, looking at a countryside that has no bearing on the things she likes and loves. He is driving through Iowa, and all she wants is the Florida sun. Cornstalks and open road, compared to luxurious homes and sandy beaches.

As the conversation strikes throughout the trip, she is impressed with his ability to hold her attention. If it was a phone conversation, the driver would have her wide open, just like the way he has his car and foot on the pedal. No phone is present and as she laughs, she looks; there is no connection physically with him or the car he claims as his pride and joy.

Exit signs come and pass. The white lines in the highway are speeding by faster and she is getting sicker. Finally enough is enough; any longer and he will feel that he is exactly what she needs. His mind converses with his heart; he is impressed with her beauty and soulfulness. He knows it was a stretch, but the opportunity was there and he took it. He looks at her as they near the next city. She sleeps against the window, but as she lies, she showcases angelic features that mesmerize him. He notices the twitch in her slumber. She is uneasy and it shows. He prepares himself for the worst, realizing that they are different in traits.

As she wakes, she looks at him and informs him that they need to talk. He much obliges, but tells her that he needs the floor first. He informs her that he will continue with the trip, but that he has to make several stops along the way and it is best for them to meet up later. With her now confused, almost baffled, he continues to tell her that he has booked her ticket to an ocean-based destination so she can lodge and relax. It hurts him to spew these words out his mouth to the fair lady who incorporates all he needs and ever wanted. She agrees, never getting a chance to speak her mind. He drops her off at the airport, watching from the road as the jets take off. Jet setting, she is off to her comfort zone. She understands that he was the right person to get her to a certain destination; but, in the end, she was more adaptable to short trips through the friendly skies than long road trips through the continent. Personality was everything, and she holds on to that. Yet, the makeup of his custom automobile just didn't have the features and body lines of what she desired, what she craved, in a vessel.

Engulfed in Time and Love

Some of us are engulfed with time, infatuated with love. Both unable to be measured after their distance of essence are too far to be diagramed. Countless acts of strategic equations formulate a hypothesis to be named after. For common law, it is the unwilling effort to give your all to feel, smell, and gravitate toward the positive energy that has you building property on "Cloud 9" for permanent residency. We blind ourselves with the thought of moral forever; unable to be created, but materialized in anyone that has loved. Never does the thought of an ending circulate in the cognizance of individuals. To create a departure plan is to percolate the understanding that what's before you isn't what's divinely created for you.

Confident in your revelations that the connection for your spouse is genuine, nothing except something unearthly can break the hold of hearts fastened by love. Perpendicular words start to rotate and become parallel on a plain. The gap between the two entities cannot allow the never before unseen into their world to disrupt the flow of energy. Once something is incorporated between these two, a multiverse will begin to formulate. The world that they saw is now depicted in a new light, with more energy sources than imagined. Time is now incomputable, while love is held onto by the smallest fibers that once intertwined the soulful hearts of both parties. With a bigger and vibrant universe to be seen, if not spiritually connected, one will depart to roam the free world, leaving a lonely source of love behind to fend off the mental and physical departure of a love so sweet.

Transversals keep the two connected, able to communicate and see one another from time to time. Yet, what was engineered by the two is no more. The property that has foundation laid on "Cloud 9" is cracked with structural damage from falling and thrown down walls. The roofline was in place, but never installed, giving the universe the ability to cast a storm that flooded love into the streets of the city with diluted competency. The stream of stormy rain mixed with love trickles off the edges of the cloud and falls downward till gravity and surface unite again. As the stream grows from the last drops falling from the sky, the sun hardens the substance to form structure. The creation of a new being is transforming as time begins to make full circular revolutions around clocks and calendars.

The love may be lost from old things and people that came and went, but the healing power of time allocates enough distance to the evolution of leftover mass. For the left-out person, they are like a foldamer. With part of their essence gone, they take artificial molecules to mimic the new ability to conquer this feat into a well-defined conformation. Standing alone in a world they roam, they are radiant from wisdom, growth and humbleness from days lost. The goodness of their hearts still shines daily. The love to love still incorporates the soulful realm of their corpse. Acceptance of beauty and understanding of self.

Love and time are collectively conjoined by the spiritual existence of both. Neither are able to be remotely diagramed as a definition or a righteous equation. Combined together, they have no limit. For when love is the connection between two people, there isn't days, months, minutes, hours or even years that can ever calculate the relevance they have on the outfit. As long as time allows breath in one's lung, then to love is to live. Therefore, if love enters into your life, the allowance of time to showcase its timeline is a blessing. I'm infatuated with love, for to love is to feel the spiritual bind that mortality can't give. I'm engulfed with the existence of time, for the interval between the start and end of life calculates my relevance by the love that I dispersed through my spirit. Love supersedes time because forever is infinite. Forever in love is spiritual.

Rolling the Dice

I rolled the dice for her, took my game of life and gambled for the jackpot. Boy, I had those cubes skipping and hopping till they came to a stop. Point after point, I hit; it was like magic on a beautiful Vegas night. I crapped out a few times, didn't get my stance right before I flicked and rolled the dice against the rails, thereby losing the small bet I had placed. I didn't invest much in the play; the house asked if I wanted to play it back. Maybe I should've walked away with the little change I had, but I knew more earnings would come. I stood and played.

When I got tired feet, they brought me a chair. Constant refills of beverages must have dislodged my reasoning. Man, I spent hours at that table. I wanted that jackpot and she smiled at me like she wanted it, too. I'm constantly throwing numbers; the crowd behind me was celebrating and screaming. Blindsided by the joy, we didn't see the pit boss sweating, a disappointed reaction to my virtues. He tried to tally me out, reasoning with me to walk away a winner. Every time I kissed those dice against those table buffers, that jackpot kissed me back passionately.

"The hell with it!" I yelled. "I'm beating the house on this roll." I sent those blocked things down that table time after time, and got close. But the dice seemed to always be cocked on someone's beating chip, turning to another point. Strategically thinking, they brought down the jackpot and put her inches next to my frame. Allowed her to kiss and whisper sweet nothings in my ear, like a warm pillow on the other side of my bed. When she got done talking, chills ran through my body. As she kissed me on my lips, I was all hers.

I prayed, "Lord, send me an angel," as I pushed all I had unto the betting field. Hell, I even got down on one knee and asked her to take my last name. She said, "Yes!" in front of everyone. She hugged me, kissed me, and planned for the future. I turned, smiling, set my feet, and threw my life down that green mile. All eyes were on me as I gambled with life, the luster of shine, the glitter of gold. Yet, the warmth in my soul cooled along the last pass of the hopping cubes.

I prayed for the jackpot, but He spoke to me. I cried for that jackpot, but He dried those tears. I fasted for that jackpot, and He provided the after meals. The dice eventually stopped, and it was a sure hit for my winnings. People bent over in awe as they slowed to a screeching halt. One die boldly presented the number four, as the other found refuge on the number three. Sick to my stomach, I hung my head. My beautiful jackpot rubbed my back, with a look that said, "Better luck next time!" Moving ahead into the crowd, she found love in the next high roller, seducing him like an ecdysiast parading a stage with one prop.

I walked away in sorrow, exhausted, but refreshed it was over. Upset with how the story ended. Hands in my pocket, I walked, and my head lifted as my fingers gripped a few stashed chips. A slot machine in the distance, a new jackpot, and resurgence for another chance showcased in my smile. One more, and I'm finished. One pull, and the machine lit up as two 7s showed their faces. One more to go! I see her face, and she is smiling at me. It's slowing down; here it comes! I see the tail of what could be the final 7. As it slows, I close my eyes--a new crowd and a new jackpot. She grabs my hand and says, "I've been waiting on you." As I open my eyes, I look first at her, not the machine. I notice her tears. A genuine connection is met as the crowd looks on. Pandemonium erupts. Music plays. Confetti falls and people scream. I thank the Lord for another chance as I kiss my consort.

A Midnight Day

The old folks say that nothing good happens after the clock strikes midnight. But, midnight only truly represents the separation of old to invite the new. Memories of yesteryear fade as the company of new opportunity presents itself. Time has this funny way of inserting people in an area to bring forth innovation and epiphanies. Mild conversation from one side of a room can migrate into an ear hustler's drums. Simple lines of questioning transgress into consideration of future attraction with two unlikely strangers. Yet, a persistent approach could warrant the services of a beauty's sleeping corpse to fully function in the wee moments of the witching hour.

The Graham Bell device now carries fiber optic waves through towers that instantly connect a wolverine to a rolling tide to converse in angelic language. Communication starts with the sincerest apology on his behalf, for to wake a fair maiden out of sleep wasn't in his nightcap for the evening. She obliges and they both, though not seen, smile at one another as the stars tilt downward, facing toward earth. It was something about the conference that they had that night, sealed with demolition utensils, for the two to break down barriers. Over the days, it would be too staggering to compile the data of so many views that intersected to showcase they were walking on the same lines for traits needed within a significant other. Charismatic smiles, coupled with witty replays, harness the vehicle they use on the path they have chosen. They know not where it leads, but they know that the air's current engulfs them in the sweetest scent that has not been smelled in years.

Distance seems minute, though their want to be in each other's presence grows chronic daily. Ultimatums are eased into daily talks as the fondness grows. A docket must be prepared instead of an infinite countdown of days with no appointment scheduled for future physical interactions. So for now, they talk, release their smiles into the atmosphere, and lay in one spot. Maybe the direction is the same, and the one star they speak to connect them like a transversal sent from the heavens. Still captions and photos release a mist of enchantment in the air, like the dusk that transforms a wretch into the goddess she has always been.

Midnight brought forth new day, new hope to a situation that never cracked the glass that my faith filled. As days proceeded and observation of what is happening occurs, they never talk past the clock striking twelve. Why seal connection when the envelope and message has just been opened and read? For this feeling, I will forever sleep before the hands align. Forever sleep in days that are allotted in time. Forever stargaze and speak aloud. Forever keep my heartbeat in faith as my soul I daily lay down.

Left, Right ... Love

I sit left of **Love**; **Love** is positioned right in the path of my acceptance. **Love** extends its left arm with opened hand. I extend my right hand and intertwine our fingers. The comfortable, soft connections of the fingers lock the foundation of acceptance together. **Love's** head pivots left as mine pivots right. Piercing eyes gaze together to release thoughts greater than a thousand words of passion.

Slight movements from **Love** ease her head forward. Compliant with the action, I, too, lean forward. The smallest of measurements block us from allowing the soft tissues of our face to connect. Piercing eyes are suddenly eclipsed, and the passion of **Love's** lips against mine sends off the acceptance of **Love's** love. My left arm still dangles freely, just as her right arm hangs exposed. Carefully, I place my left on **Love's** right. My open hand now finds refuge on **Love's** right shoulder blade.

Love places her right around my left, now open, right hand, setting up camp on the left hemisphere of my back. We pull closer; the air between our two frames is now depleted. Our heads tilt to the right simultaneously at a 135-degree angle. We begin to breathe the same air. We are one and one in love. The passion that is shared is magnified by the union. I sit at the right of **Love** as she sits at the left of me. We sit, conjoined together as one. We have collectively Left the past to create a blueprint for the Right future. In God, we trust. Through that, in love, we live.

Face Time

You did something to me last night. We found a way to secretly lie in each other's bed. You were in your element, sitting so comfortably on your soft comforter, as you comforted me. I couldn't do anything but lay there … smile and blush at the essence of beauty. You spoke to me softly. Your voice chilled me as you choreographed sentences to reflect your love of me. I stared into your eyes, paralyzing this moment as I walked over your shell with my sight. I felt your smile. The warmth of your lips felt great once I closed my eyes to envision the passion they furnish.

We're separate, separate in realms, but equal in connection. Retina display eliminates eye redness, but I cry for you with clear eyes for this love. I kiss glass screens that show your frame, but disabled the physical touch feature. We talk all night. Your facial expressions are seen as you modestly fall deeper into love's abyss. Last night, I took a bite out of "Apple." It opened my eyes to conversations socialized with futuristic characteristics. I applaud Jobs' technology; it brought distance into my personal space. It took the four walls and a locked door, which confined our rooms and fumigated it with love, to coat the atmosphere. Allowed the lights to appear dim in the backdrop, creating the perfect ambiance. Yet, still frames of my love grace the screen, leaving me in awe.

We hold hands not, no kissing or touching during this magical night. Our eyesight and dialogue yields nurturing of our hearts last night. The free elements of comfortably nestled shells were displayed. We found a way to stay in the fine print of restrictions. We found a transversal to connect one another to indirect worlds. We shrunk the world into a smaller dimension. Ensuing ticks of love's clock tock away to invite morning into this amalgam. We talked the morning sun into its daily position. We face time the night into day, face time love into our humble aboded hearts. We beat the system of wanting to be together as our device screens served as a loving depiction to grant passing authority.

Hopefully Not Just Words

I've been away from love, but I long for her touch. Her grace blankets me from my transgression. She works harder than anticipated to showcase her affection. I gaze in teary eyes that try to hold back the emotions that she is consumed with. She wonders my stance. Well, baby I stand with outreached arms. I stand in a pool of my sorrows, which I evacuated to purify this relationship. I stand firm on love, firm on the desires that the prayers we pray are coming true. I stand with sorrow of not moving in the moment like people wish I would have. But I tell you, my heart is warm and it's coming.

I wish things worked like a clock, precise and routine. Yet, I lose myself in you so many days that I'm glad your infinite love allows me to find us in your heavenly ways. I prayed a prayer with you as we held one another. That prayer I prayed released an emotion in me that I can never explain. You held my hand. I wish I could have cried physically, yet the soulful joy wept a river that ran onto the streets to vegetate our seeds sown. In the midst of you allocating your time to prepare your blessing of the law, I stand with you. As you prepare yourself to excel your life, I plan to excel ours. Align your prayer with me still and meet me at the Lord's footstool with the same desires. Let Him see fit in His eyes to anoint our vessels as one. Confirmation is our goal; conjoined till death does us part is my asking grace.

I love you unconditionally. In no way, shape or form do I want you to think that I don't want to be with you or take the next step. I pray daily and nightly. I know confirmation is coming. I'm not asking for anything but to have faith. Not in me, for I am merely human. But, in the Lord, that our prayers will be answered. You mean everything to me. I just need you to focus and show out with a smile on your face. I love you, beautiful. Thank you for this opportunity

Old Baggage, New Relationship

I see you lurking, hiding behind objects to be a chameleon while in one's presence. You have been searching for an outlet, feeding for a speedy recovery as you try to torment. I thought you were gone, removed, bagged and thrown away, like the weekly trash. I was wrong, naïve in my process, to think that I could mold life away from you so that you can find a home in a landfill miles away. I moved her, transported her into a different vicinity away from the common traffic that you once caused to create traffic jams in her life. It was before me, but it plagues me like the hurt she had to overcome.

She bagged your things up and we placed them by the door. She released your hold and I mopped her spilled heart up. You scared her life, and I found her in a state of depression, with wanting to love at the forefront. She gave me her address, and I knocked daily against that door until the entrance opened for me. She answered emotionally in a housecoat, slippers dragging her feet, and an undone head of hair that hung from her slumping neck. Beautiful as a person, her aura was majestic of a princess, once spoken to. We talked for hours in the beginning and she opened up about you. The plummeting of my heart, the burning in my soul could not describe the conviction she had in her voice about your diabolical ways.

I reach for her and she jumps. I yell through rooms and she freezes. I held her and prayed, and emotions while sleeping haunted her to the brink of crying at night. I promised her a castle, a storybook with a crown jewel on her left ring finger. A man of my word, I am there with a diamond swallowing her top side, resting on a band of smaller ones. We prepare for our future. We walk in the streets as she radiates the universe. Dark days were obsolete as she rained sunshine constantly. For so long, eye to eye was seen.

We are in love, love I tell you. And I be damned if the past will break this bond. She loved you, cared for you, stepped over people to get to you. And what you do? Abused her, mentally raped her, and violently tortured her with acidic words that cooked holes into her soul. I prayed for her! Sacrificed my life for her! Gave up on just enough to have her come in my life to provide abundance! And you! You waltz back in, strutting like a Clydesdale freshly groomed in a parade. Your image isn't invisible to me. I remember you from the portraits that she stained in my mind of hurt. Those bags I thought I dumped, yeah I must have mixed some of the confines with some of our valuable things. Hung you on a shelf, put you in a closet, or packed you in the basement.

We're close and I'm getting ready for forever with her. The dates are rolling off the calendar and the ceremony is approaching. The look in her eyes, I see the dwindling twinkle fall. Her demeanor alters here and there to a mundane state of affairs. We're around the block from our destination, and I will get out and walk to Heaven if it's that close. She's throwing things in frantic, cursing from frustrations that are easily fixable. She yells at me for being too nice, for the backbone she swears I don't have any more. The things I feel she deserves are mere trinkets and don't glow her pretty smile like previous.

As I pray, she wrestles from the voice of the Lord, speaking back to me, "You have crawled into a threesome." My Lord prepares me for battle, gives me instructions with intricate findings for me to master. Nestled in my armor, like an Ephesian, I stand valiantly for you to show your serpent head. You can't bribe her with the riches of the world when my Lord dwells in the Heavenly ranks. As she sleeps and I exorcise your demon tonight, understand I shall bury your corpse and kill your soul. Our life is an honor, a gift from my Lord to us as He died for our sins. As morning comes, she will yawn and find me up and cleaning our castle. Bags by the door, she will look in confusion as the trash has already been taken this week. A knock on the door, I will pick them up and unlock the gateway. As she peeks her head around the wall, a smile will light up her face again as I hand the tribulation to our Lord.

The Things She Does for Me

She cries for me; her eyes send streams profusely down her cheeks when she is overwhelmed with love. She is in love with me; words can't formulate the emotions she has for me. She prayed for me. Thoughts of settling only crossed her mind as the Lord delivered me to her. She is happy with me. The stares of admiration send chills to me. She smiles so deeply; the joy she encompasses is breathtaking to witness. She cares for me. The protection of my heart is guarded by this soldier of God. She lives for me. The undeniable promise of being complete in the Lord. She dwells with me. Her spirit touches mine as we pray collectively for one another.

She lies with me. The mutual foundation of a future in the Lord's eyes. She explains to me the inner workings of how her heart hugs her soul to bring tearful cries. She rests in me. I lift the weight of her world off her shoulders, whenever I can help. She counts on me to play the role of provider. Security is adorned on me. She is confused by me. Repeatedly, she wonders where I came from, suddenly making her dreams a reality. She compliments me. She carries her own completion in Christ. If God sees fit, we unionize in His presence. She fits with me. Everything is in place; compromise isn't used to discover our next step. She dreams with me. The plans and discussions have been spoken upon as we catch up with our future. She believes in me. We push the bar of success higher together as achievements are met. She is everything to me. All I want and all I need to live out my days. Beyond worldly love, into agape love, through our Lord and Savior, Jesus Christ, who is first in our life as one.

How I Feel Right Now

This is unexplainable love, forecasted by the Lord to shower goodness to my soul. I can't fathom the words to create the right definition. The imagery that is in front of me is more breathtaking than anything I envisioned. I write about this type of love. I will lose my pen's ink in the praying characteristics of my heart's desires. My faith agent was sent out; he rested at the footstep of the Lord. He waited for instructions on a time, place, and person. That agent of mine placed me in the company of a rib, stayed alongside me until the conversation yielded future memories in both eyes. Now my agent peruses the future, confirming the guided steps of the Lord by bring my future into present interaction of blessed gifts.

This was too much for me to handle, so I prayed. I needed the Lord to intervene with a message of goodness and mercy for my soul. For so long, I looked out my window of life and saw her, but the Lord opened a door for the two of us to enter each other's world. My body stays restful on limited hours of sleep. The catching up of hearts' connections has us up till the morning entrance periodically. Completely different from anything we have ever had before, the delicate fibers of this relationship are intertwined with the blessings of the Lord. I'm not careless, reckless, or insensitive with this precious gift. We pray nightly, collectively and individually. The Lord is the head of our lives; we started early with Him being the head of our future household. All burdens of past relationships are removed as we join as two complete individuals in Christ.

The admiration is keen, preciously mastered and engineered for the trials and tribulations of worldly warfare. The effect she has on me is astonishing; the twinkle in my eyes has the company of a vibrant smile and an upbeat attitude, to say the least. She cares for my wellbeing; she elevates my transgressions through spoken words given to her spiritually to sit them in the Lord's hands. We speak of the future. Time is moving and we look forward to the covenant. We are selfish; we want all of each other, yet even more of the Lord. Captured pictures are still portraits of glowing faces within God's mercy. I once thought my helpmeet died at birth. Then, I grew in the Lord's eyes and was granted with heavenly speech to manifest my maturity through communication and kill my childish ways. My dialect is now filled with the placement of Scripture to understand my life's testimonies.

I am in awe over this, pure goodness sealed with a forehead kiss from the Lord. We both kneel before Him, awaiting confirmation. I wake with love on my mind. I travel daily with love around me. I sleep with love next to me to get through the night. As love soaks in all my breaths of life, I thank you, Lord, multiple times a day. My words are filled. My heart is freed, as my soul is nestled in the bosom to stay consumed in your presence, oh, Lord.

Sealed Prayer

I looked in the sky and saw the clouds part.

The sky turned blue as the light broke the dark.

I stood by myself as one, and prayed for two.

Closed my eyes to seal the prayer, and then there was you.

Breathtaking beauty, it reflected off you with colors.

Selfish in my ways, I wanted you as my lover.

You as my wife. You as my life.

You to hold my hands as we soar to new heights.

To be the representation of me, and me to you;

For you to be the miracle that houses my miracle of three from two.

To stand together through the storms that brew;

To hold each other nightly as a new day comes through;

To kiss a sweet kiss that's passionate to our touch;

To never want for nothing because reality isn't enough.

No person can separate the heavens' gift to me.

I make a beloved promise that I am all the man you dreamt me to be.

After the Prayer

We're apart; disconnected by touch, but nestled together spiritually. I wonder random thoughts as the ceiling above my bed allows me to paint vibrantly on its stucco accent.

She's alone, alone in a place I'm rushing to get to. She arrived before me; released the clinched muscles of her body and allowed her lungs to breathe in the crisp air of relaxation. She is covered though, protected on her flight as the arrival to her destination is flawless. I wonder her locale. If I could speak to her right now, without interruption, I surely would.

I smile while all alone, yet worry in the same sense as terror lurks behind every corner of this picture reel. I close my eyes to force my mind to rest; I know she is checking the time, proposing that I stood her up. Yet, I'm coming for you, baby, to hold your hand and affectionately cascade around for all to see.

I'm almost there! If only I could get my heart to stop pounding beats that have my eardrums signaling new thoughts to my sporadic mind!

She should have told me of her dream place tonight. No location on my flight ticket; just arrival time if the comic weather holds constant without further delay.

The clock is ticking; the seconds of allotment have the hands of time moving at a feverish pace.

I'm late! My baby is all alone in a foreign place dreamt upon, where I have no control of her protection.

Shut down, body! Allow me to rest my weary eyes that have seen too much of life for this one day. Allow me to enjoy night by awarding the companionship of love.

My muscles are lax; my comfort is wrapped in the blanket that warms my shell. I cradle the pillow draped in her scent and engulf all the fragrance she left prior so I can be closer to all of her.

I finally found her! Staring at me with her deep eyes, she blushes.

"I've been waiting for you," she utters in the softest sentence. Mesmerized by love, I explain my tardiness. She cares less of the reason and more of how I located her tonight.

As she leans close for a kiss, my answer whispers passionately into her left ear as the measurements of touch get minimal.

"I've waited a long time for the reality of true love. I couldn't fathom losing you in our dreams."

Kindred Spirits

It's tranquil in the house, kindred spirits attached to the essence of love. Bringing forth conversations to the Lord, various steps insinuate proper movements along the plights in life. The voices are connected and the growth spiritually is highlighted in speech. They dwell in the realm of the Lord as they pray for a constructed covenant, which one day, is granted. The skilled thinking of two scholars has them running through passages of the "Good Book" for references.

The lines of communication are open: two on the phone, with the Lord serving as operator, listening to the servants and smiles. They release their thoughts; they speak of their hearts' desires. The body of his has been worked upon as he now rests after weary days. Her shell has been formed and from him, she is completed from his side. They awake in the Lord's eyes, collectively made for one another in the image of the Lord. A plentiful harvest awaits them; the connection they house is stronger than any emotion. They fit; complete in the Lord, they walk a road that will grant them a heavenly love that plays chords of joy. Prosperity is all around their vision, able to approach tomorrow differently for the future is solidifying itself daily. They meet their end of the heavenly bargain constantly. They are God's servants in the Lord's image, an image that will grant a union that no man can tear apart once commenced by a shepherd of the Lord. Completion is in the Lord, and in the Lord they dwell.

I'm Not Worthy

She was it! I mean she possessed variables that cracked my Davinci Code daily. Morning sun broke the sky as we conversed meaningfully into each other's ears. She touched my soul despite the distance which separated our bodies. I prayed for something like this, but was I ready?

I daydreamed about her glowing skin. Her smile that brings sunshine. Her ability to understand the life I own. We sat on park benches, listening to the waves hit the rocks. We stared into each other's eyes in mesmerizing fashion. She loved to run, so I ran alongside her, ensuring myself she would never run off with my heart.

That same heart softened. It pumped blood that wanted to choose life over stagnate retribution. Was she *love*? That love I only dreamt and heard the old folks speak of. Was she the bearer of the finger in need of my diamond, the one which I would bleed my soul dry to present to the right person?

It was too early, but the question lingered. I respected her placement in my life and never allowed her to stay late into the night. I approached this situation with the Lord on my side instead of my roaming red eye as navigation. I remember like it was yesterday--the night I finally gave *love* my all, without distractions from my ego.

We sat nestled next to each other, watching television. She looked like a goddess from a dream that was reoccurring since childhood. I stroked her hair as she closed her eyes and smiled. I kissed her lips and felt the passion in the room retreat the demons that latched onto me. The way we seductively danced with clothes on sent warning signals to areas of our bodies that didn't understand the command, "Stop!" She once told me she was waiting on marriage to allow the next man to penetrate her. I heard her, but the way the aroma coated the room, I wanted her to wrestle me with both sets of lips and engulf me inside her.

We pushed the envelope a little further. Russian hands found themselves rubbing each other's body parts. I was trying to refrain from the sinful thoughts, which pumped blood into sections where her clothed body now sat atop. Her hair flipped in my face, my hands raked the smalls of her back. I wanted to stop to protect the good girl in her, but she chose to let the bad seed have its way. If sin wanted a show to watch, we were giving it all we had at that moment.

We rose and headed to the bedroom, thoughts spiraling around in my head. Kissing with my eyes open, I saw love allowing sin to kill what heaven may have ordained. I'm confused! Am I about to rationalize right from wrong? Am I about to eliminate the title opportunist from my description?

I released my lips from hers and asked, "Are you sure about what's next?"

Her seductive, yet simple response was, "Yes."

I passionately kissed her some more, a bulging section of my pants awaiting parole like an incarcerated inmate. That's when I pulled back to look her deep in her eyes.

"I want you! All of you! I want to give you every inch you can handle. But I'm not worthy," I uttered in confusion.

"Excuse me…" she replied. "I am not worthy to have you at this moment."

I spoke one more time. I was more than ready to give her a night of passion, but I wasn't the man at that moment to burrow inside her and write my name on her walls with flaw. Bewildered and shocked, her eyes smiled from her cemented lips. She stood in front of me, housing the silhouette I saw in my dreams. Reality was upon me, but tonight wasn't *the night.*

I walked to her car with limited words. I opened the door and turned her toward me. I kissed her passionately once more, hoping her knees would get weak and it would be enough to cause her to come back.

As she drove off, I closed the door to my house and asked myself, "Who was that speaking for me? I'm not worthy?" I had no idea why I said this, as I replayed the scene repeatedly in my mind. Could this be *love?* Was there more I had to do to show myself deservingness? I smiled as I cleaned my house, hoping one day to make it a home fit for her.

To Whom It May Concern

I found it! That feeling when separation meets anxiety. You are the mimicking feeling of incompleteness when away because completion lies on the other side of the equal sign when we're added together. You're that occurrence that collapses one's lungs into making it hard to breathe without each other. It's the completion of self-worth through the eyes of your soul mate. I stare in those eyes, down the corridors of immature love, and patiently remove brick by brick the wall you have up from your past.

You're in my grip. I'm holding love with my soul wrapped around her heart. I'll lay all my cards on the table for you. Let you dissect my intricate workings and learn my encrypted code. I'll give you my last and set out to provide you more, just to take care of home till I secure our forever.

I dreamt of you when my lust out beat my heart. I wondered where you were while I felt the warmth of another woman's womb. I silenced my lust, while I vocalized my love. I'm far from blemish-free, but I will bathe in angel tears to rebirth myself as the protector of your forever. I once loved to dance with the devil, until you came along. Now, I long for your forever and the security of only your body to hold.

Wake me with your lips, the softest peace offering of Heaven I know. Smile when we lock eyes, and allow my pupils to showcase my admiration for this moment. Talk to me in various tones, tones that tell me what makes me inferior to the other guys that couldn't unlock your future. Caress my body with your gentle hands. Rub out my inequities that each day brings. Set goals for our future. Let's build a legacy with half of your traits and half of mine.

I'm talking in circles to an empty left hand, which tells the public you aren't spoken for. I'm far from speaking for you, but close to claim property on Cloud 9 for forever with you. You're it! I mean, I'm set in my ways like a solitaire on infused malleable metals. What I'm trying to hint at is your ring finger needs some weight on it. Secretly, I'm paving foundation on a plot of land for us. Technically, I'm writing to release all my thoughts to you in scribe so you can read them after I take a knee. I want you to understand more of me and allow me to crown you my queen.

Today, I asked your family for your hand in marriage and they approved. My plan is simple. You're first over everything in this world after God. Your heart needs protection, so let me be your king. Our family will need me to make provisions daily. I want you to touch and agree that we unite as one and stand tall as we face this world, with our backs to it and our commitment in Heaven. Just love me like the thought of losing me gives you an anxiety attack. Dwell with me in the open, holding hearts like hands. Rest with me nightly, holding fast to prayers for a new day to fall in love all over again with the sun breaking the sky on our windowpane.

With Your Blessing

Long days have come to a sunset close with me lunging on one knee in front of the love of my life. A princess cut solitaire with a trail of diamonds to make up her infinity band. Family and friends look on in the distance as they anticipate the joy of her saying, "Yes!" Her feet in heels. Her frame in an elegant dress. Her hair, face and nails done for pictures after the tears fall from her initial reaction to my question. She's all I need to conquer the world in front of me. I want to be all she wants to spend her days with going forward.

There was just one thing to do to make this a reality: ask her family for their blessing.

I never approached a man to ask him to relinquish his protective covering he held over his daughter. I played with words and tone repeatedly as I imagined the way the conversation would play out. Surely, I put my time in to showcase my worthiness. Surely, I exemplified the making of the man they could see their child being happy with for the rest of her life.

Maybe I wasn't the one, in their eyes. Maybe they thought I was a summer breeze that lasted through the winter months. They could have vetted someone already, and I could have just been someone who was tolerated until the families orchestrated the arrangement. Maybe they felt like I was the smile on her face, but far from the beat in her heart. Maybe they thought I could possibly provide versus potentially providing if they said, "Yes!" They needed definite answers for their child.

That's when I realized I was in the audition of my life this whole time. I lived in a way that no record from my early years followed me to my future. Any water under my bridge washed my past away, like I baptized my soul in the murky water and emerged spotless. I walked an unbeaten path to pave a way for myself. I hold no regrets. I still wonder if there is a blemish somewhere that may derail this next move in life.

Clouded mind with mumbling words, I tried to formulate the meeting. Her parents understood what was coming, but never knew when the day would come. The way they insinuated during casual conversation left me staring at the ceiling for answers. When they drilled with questions, I knew she was a great girl, but the answers they looked for didn't quite flow out my mouth. I wanted love for life, to be with someone that would awake me in the morning with kisses of new life. I wanted my existence to break generational miscues that found their way into my world. I couldn't answer their questions directly because I was still confessing my love.

The plot thickened. The air I inhaled shortened my breath as time progressed. The love was building, but time was ticking on the patience of the uncrowned queen. She rarely engaged in conversations to pinpoint a timeframe, but she did play mind games to see where I was in my commitment to her. Staring in her eyes, and seeing them wanting me forever, drained my soul as I knew I was close.

She deserved the world, and when that diamond graced my eyesight, I saw our tomorrow on her finger before it ever had a setting.

She didn't loan me her heart, nor allow me to play in her secret garden to trample her vegetation. She didn't French kiss me with passion to have me kiss and tell. She entrusted me to honor the words I spoke face to face, those words I whispered softly in her ear. I needed to purchase the world and present the crown on her finger for clarity clearer than the stone itself.

I sit across from her father and engage in conversation that will define his respect for me. Chest up, with a tone that shows no fear, I walk down my thoughts on why me. He listens and slowly shakes his head. We engage in direct eye contact as he positions he focus back on me. Then, he utters:

"My daughter is my heart, my seed that has blossomed into a beautiful woman. I understand your intentions and, as a man, I respect you for coming to me for her hand. Over the years, you have proven to us that you can not only handle her, but also give her the universe if it was available. We admire the way you love on her, and you have my blessing to have my baby's hand in marriage."

With the weight lifted off my back, I stood and extended my hand. With a smile on his face, he grabbed my hand and pulled me close. The embrace let me know my fate was sealed. As I left, all I could think about was how I was about to propose to the love of my life. However it was about to be, the anxiety to get it right was now looming large.

A Perfect Evening

A cell phone rings with the ring tone of his woman's favorite song. He answers with the happiest voice, "Hey, honey! How is work?"

She immediately barrels constant discomfort about the activities that happened in her day to make her irate.

He listens without reply. He knows that this is her moment to vent, to reincarnate these events and ask for understanding. She says she is physically tired of the same scenarios daily, same actions from co-workers that set off her same reactions.

Minutes go by. As she approaches the close of telling about her frustrating day, she realizes she hasn't showed her man any verbal affection—just constant rambling of daily reoccurring events.

She abruptly stops to say, "I'm sorry, honey. How is your day?"

Assuring her that his day was fine, he asks her if there was anything in his power he could do to make the rest of her day wonderful.

She replied, "Just you listening and being you is all I need!"

Realizing that she is an attractive, educated, well-rounded woman, he constantly has to set new precedence. The biggest fear for him is the introduction of complacency.

Nothing more nerve wrecking than thinking there isn't any more growth to their relationship.

As he drives home, he plays various ways in his head that could possibly bring satisfaction to his queen's world. He wanders back and forth mentally, adding and subtracting ideas that will work, along with those that will be less expecting and bring honor back to her day.

The conception of the plot nears completion. He stops numerous times at several shops to bring reality to the illusion he premeditated happening that night. He glances down at his watch and calculates the time remaining to his delicate surprise.

As he enters his abode, he surveys the perimeters to make sure everything is tidy and in place. He doesn't want anything to alter her attention from the evening that awaits her.

With time rapidly aging, he cleans all the rooms, over-indulging in the master bedroom and bathroom. He cleans these two areas with the eye of a hawk, for he knows these will be the two rooms that will house the majority of their time.

Between rooms, he incorporates time to prepare a preferred dish he knows will gain her acceptance. Crafting the meal, he sets the dish to simmer as he returns to the two rooms to position the items that will highlight the extra touch of love.

Time winds down and the phone rings. It's his supporting actress, informing him of her position on her route home. Angelically, she asks if there was anything she needs to stop and pick up. Not knowing that in just minutes, she wouldn't have to move another muscle.

She approaches their home and instantly realizes four key lights on in the house. Not knowing what awaits her inside, she makes her own assumption, thinking in her head that her man is just trying to light up the entire block.

As she inserts her key into the keyhole, the door is helpingly pushed open. Her king instantly says, "Hello," and kisses her ever-so softly on her lips.

"Let me take your bags," he says, smiling. He turns and walks away, as she starts a sentence.

"Why are all the lights on in the house? You can see them from two blocks away."

As her bags are placed next to the couch, he apologetically says, "I am sorry, honey. I will cut them off immediately." She walks around the corner that separates the two, just as he is approaching the light switch in the dining room. Simultaneously, the lights go off as she enters the room.

She stands in amazement as she cases the room, looking at the decorative arrangement that showcases the prepared meal. Instantly, a tear falls as she gazes at the blinking candles that illuminate the room. The placement of the candle holder gravitates the light toward an arrangement of multicolored roses right in front of her seat at the table.

Walking over to him, she says with a tearful voice, "I love you."

With an emotional embrace, he whispers in her ear, "Just as quick as your day turns dark, your night can brighten." He wipes the tears off her cheeks and escorts her to her reserved place setting.

As he prepares her meal, she is still overwhelmed by the preparation he put into the evening. Gingerly placing the food into her mouth due to the hotness of the freshly done entree, she savors every spice that was used to flavor the meal.

Staring up at her man, she thanks him again for releasing the tension she allowed to build up. He, in turn, makes it very clear there is no need for thanks. Taking her hand as he helps her out of her seat, he insinuates she needs to take her work clothes off and slip into something more comfortable.

They proceed down the corridor that leads to the master bathroom. Amazed and shocked, she now notices small candles and rose petals. Beautiful to sight, the light and the roses make the gazed hardwood flooring heaven to walk on.

Pivoting around the threshold of the bathroom, more tears are generated as she analyzes the height of the bubble bath and the reflection of the lit candles. The aroma that enters her nose feels smoother than silk on the softest skin.

He places her on a foot stool, still holding her hands, as he kneels down in front of her. She bends over to hug him, but he draws back and tells her to relax.

Slipping her garments off, he walks over to the back of the door to get a fresh towel for when she gets out of the bath. He walks over and wraps the towel around her, placing a knot right beneath her left breast. She kisses him and proceeds toward the tub. He watches her sashay across the road of rose petals, which leads to her relaxing exfoliations.

Enticed by the way the towel droops low in the back, the towel knot losing structure with every step, he watches it finally fall off as she sticks her right foot in the water to check the temperature.

Resting for a minute, he continues to watch as she places her hair into a ponytail and sinks into the bubble bath. The bath water is the right temperature. She notices the oils in the water, clinging to her skin. Upon further meditation, the steam releases the scent of French vanilla with a hint of peach aroma. She cracks a smile and lets the warmth of the water take her out of reality.

Tired from the preparation for his fair maiden, he takes a deep breath and proceeds to the tub. Forecasting his next action, he gets mesmerized by the tranquility she now has plastered on her face.

He sits on the tip of the tub. Leaning over, he embraces her slumber with a peck to the lips.

As her eyes open slowly, he says, "I will bathe you." He takes the face cloth and soap, merging them together to form the perfect lather. He ever so gently runs the towel across her frame.

His fingers and palm massage her with every stroke to her body. Delicately, he covers her body with soap, running his hand across and around her chest. She couldn't help but tingle from the erotic feeling he gave her. She stands and places one foot on the tub. He wipes her inner and outer thighs as she holds on by positioning her hands around his neck. After switching and washing her opposite leg, he helps her back into the water and uses the face cloth to rinse the soap off her glistening body.

Light years away from complaining at this moment in time, she admires his level of sensitivity and seduction. He escorts her back to the same foot stool, sitting her down. He grabs the lotion and gently caresses every inch of her body, just as he'd done in the tub.

The world she's in is enchanted, and her king is her servant, who moves with no commands. Her tear ducts are dry, eye lids puffed from crying. His commitment to her happiness is evident and his love is shown throughout the night.

She tries to insist and return the favor. Unwilling to agree, he stands firm and foils her new plans. Conceived spontaneously, he knows that to allow her to give back interrupts his preconceived actions. She continues to receive, understanding the thought that was put into the evening--plus the unconditional want he displays.

From the bathroom, she is led into the bedroom. The room's fragrance is mind blowing; the satin sheets are crimped with creases. Two oil burners fill the air. The inhalation of the scent, same as in the bathroom, continues to overwhelm her.

Draped barely in a towel, she sits down as the California King absorbs her weight. Eye level with her man's torso, she runs her hands up his chest and pulls his shirt over his head. His pants and belt are unbuttoned next.

They hit the floor with the conviction of the true nightcap on the evening.

He bends over. Their foreheads touch as their lips connect. He kisses lower from her lips to her neck, down to her breast. His tongue runs south like a bird migrating for winter. As he drops back down to his knees, she wraps her hand back around his head, stroking his hair and rubbing his ear.

While she awaits his next action, he finds a box that he strategically placed under the bed. He uses his finger to open it and grips the confines into his palm. As she indulges in the romance she feels, he grabs her left arm and rubs it against his body.

She accepts the notion and caresses his torso. He takes his opposite hand and slides the vibrant, light reflecting diamond onto her ring finger that seals his master plan. Her head returns from the clouds to witness the rock that bulges from her finger. The puffy, non-tearful eyes just found new irrigation from her spiritual sprinkler system.

Before he could ask, her mouth lets the world be known that it was a sure, "Yes!" Her body shook as her muscles grew tight with a hug of confirmation. With not one doubt in her mind, she pledged to be his queen; gave verbal clarification that she was his and wasn't going anywhere else.

He rose from his knees. She grabbed him and pulled him close. As she sat straight up, he applied force as her back arched. Slowly, she inched toward the sheets to bring connection. As the oil from her bath and lotion clinched the fabric, their chests pushed against one another. Their pelvises aligned. Her head rose up, only to look briefly. A sigh of relief was released just as her womb purified the connection.

He whispers, "I love you," as she migrates toward the head board. She lifts her head one last time. While crying, her lips utter the words, "Thank you," as she nibbles on his ear. She now releases all the muscles in her body as her sweat glands moisturize her body.

The evening is consummated. Her chemical reactions, tears from acceptance, and the yelling of her "Yes!" warrant the stamp of approval. Signed, sealed and delivered by the fetal position she lies in after the last thrust. He is mesmerized once again by his queen's joy. He approaches her and plants a kiss on her head, turns away and begins to clean up the decoration that left her smiling in her sleep.

About the Author

Like a classic Picasso painting, his literary genius doesn't just leap off the pages—it gets into the heart and soul of the reader. Mirroring the style and prose of literary greats such as Robert Frost, Langston Hughes and Maya Angelou, Kefentse Booth not only paints vivid pictures with his choice of words—he immerses the reader so deep into the situation at hand that they hardly ever have time to come up for fresh air. His undeniable love for music and passion for the written (and spoken) word shape his sentences into rhythmic compositions that leave readers craving more long after they've turned the last page.

Raised by a Detroit public school educator, Booth's poetic infatuation sprouted at a very young age—landing him a poetry feature in *The Michigan Chronicle*, Detroit's oldest African-American newspaper, at the age of twelve. His obsession with the concept of love, coupled with his strong interest in community affairs and social conscious topics, led him to compile essay-style narrations, which catapulted him into writing competitions as early as high school. Supported by teachers and family, Booth soon excelled in numerous writing contests, where he greater honed his skills and learned how to engage audiences of all diversities.

Even when he attended Tuskegee University, where he obtained his Bachelor of Science in Business Administration, Booth not only played sports consistently—

but he continued to pursue his exposition as he wrote about the parallels of love and life.

In his second book, *Stranded On Love's Highway*, Booth takes readers on a journey of life lessons and the reality of relationships. No matter where readers choose to get on this sensual highway, they will experience pain, pleasure and fiery passion—even if they only read one excerpt. Written from a personal perspective of his past mishaps, mistakes and misfits, Booth strives to intertwine the realistic, yet unexpected love life of the average reader—allowing readers worldwide to not only see themselves, but *feel* themselves in the moment.

Because of his great love for all things literary, Booth founded Street Light Dreams, LLC, where he cultivates and educates writers to pursue their passion and become published authors. He resides with his wife, Fallon, in the surrounding metropolitan Detroit area.

www.ingramcontent.com/pod-product-compliance
Lightning Source LLC
Chambersburg PA
CBHW071009120726
47910CB00004B/1442